For Tanner and Jon-Patrick
I love you to the moon and beyond
-PG

For Anna, Mickey, Ari, Mimi, Bill,
Bear and Greyson
-DM

"Stella and the Dinos…Alive in Space!"   First Edition   Published by PGulley Projects LLC

Copyright © PGulley Projects LLC - All rights reserved. This book or parts thereof may not be reproduced in any form, stored in any retrieval system, or transmitted in any form by any means - electronic, mechanical, photocopy, recording, or otherwise without prior written permission of the publisher, except as provided by United States of America copyright law. For permission requests: **stella@stellathedino.com**   ISBN 9781735292403   Manufactured in PRC

visit: **www.stellathedino.com**   follow: **@stellathedino**

STELLA AND THE DINOS
...ALIVE IN SPACE!

Written by **PEYTON GULLEY**
Illustrated by **DESI MOORE**

If no one ever told you, then I'd like to tell you now
that dinosaurs are still alive! And let me tell you how.

See, dinos have a planet, their own sun and their own place.
I'm telling you that dinos are alive in outer space.

You know that long ago on Earth the dinosaurs were king - the biggest of the animals and eating everything.

Each dinosaur was different, some on land and some with wings, with different dino interests, doing different dino things.

Some dinosaurs were athletes, some dinosaurs read books.
Some dinosaurs were quite a sight with dinosaur good looks.

Some dinosaurs took bubble baths,

...some cleaned their dino homes.

Some dinosaurs were always on their giant dino phones.

There were dancing dinosaurs and dinos who could sing.
There were lazy dinosaurs who never did a thing.

Some dinosaurs were super-fast, and some were very slow.

But there is just one dinosaur whose name you need to know.

Stella the dino scientist was only just a kid,
but dinos are alive today because of what she did.
See, Stella was a thinker, and she liked to use her mind,
exploring almost everything to see what she could find.

And every night at bedtime Stella looked into the stars
to see if she could catch a glimpse of Jupiter or Mars.

But one night, through her telescope, she saw something new,
and even genius Stella wasn't sure what she should do.

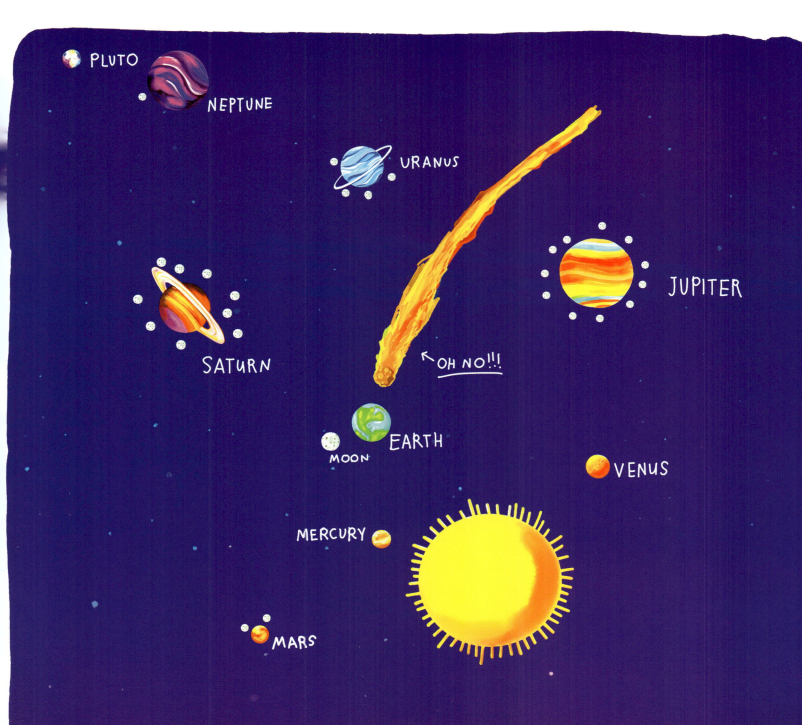

She saw a giant rock in space, and much to her dismay
the rock was headed straight for Earth and speeding on its way.

This was a disaster - Stella knew this wasn't good.
She had to spread the news around, tell everyone she could.

She warned the dino moms that their babies were in danger, but they wouldn't listen to some tiny dino stranger.

She tried to tell the dino dads the world was going to end,
but dino dads had work to do: "No time, my little friend!"

**Stella told the athletes, and she got more of the same -
"Little girl, the world is fine. You're holding up our game."**

The dinos seemed uninterested with danger on its way, but Stella couldn't give up. No, she had to save the day!

The dinosaurs needed Stella, because they didn't know an asteroid would soon arrive, and they needed to go.

But where to go?
What to do?
Then letting out a sigh,
Stella lifted up her head
and looked into the sky.

"THERE!" she shouted, filled with joy, a big smile on her face.
"I'll take all the dinosaurs to live in outer space."
So Stella built a rocket ship and finished just in time.
The asteroid got closer, and the dinos changed their mind.

Dino games were ended, dino bubble baths were drained.
Nothing good was coming for a dino who remained.

So dinosaurs, both old and young, and dinos big and small came to Stella's rocket shop, and she welcomed them all.

The dinos all apologized, admitting they were wrong.
And Stella said, "We're good, my friends! Get in and come along."

3...the countdown had begun, 2...now down below,
1...the rocket fired up and it was time to go!

The rocket shot off through the sky,
and when it passed the moon

the asteroid slammed into Earth
and made a giant BOOM.

The dinosaurs let out a cheer, so happy to survive,
"HOORAY to little Stella, she's the reason we're alive!"

Then Stella thought, "Who can say now what the future brings -
after Mars and Jupiter, and Saturn with its rings,
Uranus and then Neptune, after Pluto, who can know
where dinosaurs in space lost in a rocket ship might go?"

But, WOW! DINO ASTRONAUTS exploring the unknown,
traveling the universe until they find a home.

WHERE'D THEY GO?
WILL THEY COME BACK?
ARE THEY AROUND OUT THERE?

Could it be, today, that they are still alive somewhere?

Well, before you go to bed, look out into the stars.
Maybe you can catch a glimpse of Jupiter or Mars.
Or maybe you'll see something that is wonderful and new -
maybe there's a dinosaur who's looking back at you!

> PEYTON GULLEY IS FOREVER GRATEFUL TO THE FOLLOWING PEOPLE WHO SUPPORTED STELLA'S CREATIVE JOURNEY AND HELPED BRING HER TO LIFE:

Andrew Grieco • Andy Green • Angela Martin • Beau Trudel
Benjamin & Charlotte Pachman • Billy Mikelson • Brian Feit • Buffy Pederson
Caroline & Emily Kassie • Carlos Lopez • Casey McKerchie • Chelsi Brace • Chris Workman
Christopher Chiou • Daniel J. Powell • Darcy Boggs • Deah Gulley & Terry Miles
Derek Cupples • Ed Jordan • Erwin Torres • George Archbold • Haley Perryman
James Anderson Moore III & Karen Moore • James Anderson Moore IV • Jeanie Gulley Brown
Jennifer Cohan • Jeremy Zucker • John Jigitz • John Philp Thompson III • Jonathan Maize
Judy Moorehead • Julian Morris • Kenneth Garrett • Kyle Lui • Kyle Zink • Len Morgan
Lydia & Michael Kives • Mackenzie Gulley • Marcelo Valente • Marla & John Marks
Matt Sandler • Michael Acton Smith • Michael Hess • Nicholas Brown • Paul & Amanda Gulley
PJ Gulley • Reid Butcher • Sean Patterson • Sharon Madden • Stacy Pitman Edwards
The Colby Family • Tianta Harrison • Trevor Jacobson • Tyler Giles • Tyler Oakley